The Littles
Have a Merry Christmas

Adapted from *The Littles and the Trash Tinies* by John Peterson.
Copyright © 1977 by John Peterson.

ISBN 0-439-42498-4

12 11 10 9 8 7 6 5 4 3 2   3 4 5 6 7/0

Printed in the U.S.A.
First Scholastic printing, November 2002

The Littles Have a Merry Christmas

Adapted by **Teddy Slater**
from **THE LITTLES AND THE TRASH TINIES**
by **John Peterson**
Illustrated by **Jacqueline Rogers**

SCHOLASTIC INC.
New York   Toronto   London   Auckland   Sydney
Mexico City   New Delhi   Hong Kong   Buenos Aires

There were tiny people

with nice long tails

living all over

The Big Valley.

Tree Tinies lived in trees.

Trash Tinies lived

in the city dump.

And, of course,

House Tinies lived

in houses.

But no matter where they lived,

tiny people never let

big people see them.

It was almost Christmas,
and all the Tinies
were full of holiday
cheer...

. . . especially the Littles.

The Littles lived in

a secret apartment

inside the walls of the

Bigg family's house.

Uncle Nick had just moved in.

It was time for him to rest

after thirty years of fighting

mice in Trash City.

"Uncle Nick looks sad,"
Lucy Little said to Tom.
"I think he misses his friends
in Trash City."

"I wish we could
bring Uncle Nick's
friends here for Christmas,"
said Tom Little.
"That would cheer him up."

"But Trash City is
hidden way under the dump,"
Lucy said. "We'd never find it."
"*I* know where it is,"
Mr. Little said.
He showed them a map.

"Nick made this for
me a long time ago," he said.

That afternoon,

Mr. Little, Tom, and Lucy

stood outside in the cold.

They were waiting for

the garbage truck.

When no one was looking,

the Littles climbed

onto the truck

and hid.

The truck stopped at
every house on the
way to the dump.
Stop! Go! Stop! Go!
It was a long,
bumpy ride.

At last, they reached
the dump.

When the truck drove

away, the Littles

put up their tent

and ate a picnic

dinner.

Then they curled up
in their sleeping bags
and said, "Good night."

The next morning,
Mr. Little led the
way to Trash City's
secret entrance.

The Littles slipped
and slid down the
cold, icy pipe.
Down, down, down.

Suddenly, they shot

out of the pipe

and landed in a heap.

A crowd of tiny people

came to look at the Littles.

They were all wearing

old but neatly patched clothes.

"I'm Mayor Itsy Clutter,"

said a man in a brown hat.

"Welcome to Trash City."

The Littles told the mayor
who they were and
what they wanted.

Mayor Clutter took
the Littles on a
tour of the city.

Then he introduced
them to the Ash
family, the Bits, and
the Scraps.
They all wanted to
help Major Nick.

So did the McDust
twins, Tip and Winkie.
"Major Nick was like
a father to us,"
Tip told Tom.

That afternoon, five
tiny passengers took
the long, bumpy ride
back to the Biggs's
house.

Uncle Nick was so glad

to see the twins that

he laughed out loud.

"Ho! Ho! Ho!"

Late that night,

the tiny people tiptoed

into a dollhouse

under the Bigg Christmas tree.

"This is the perfect place
for our Christmas party,"
Uncle Nick said.
And he had a very merry
Christmas, after all.